KU-175-449

Little Bear's Visit

An **I Can Read** book

Little Bear's Visit

ELSE HOLMELUND MINARIK

pictures by
MAURICE SENDAK

HEINEMANN · LONDON

William Heinemann Ltd
Michelin House
81 Fulham Road
London SW3 6RB

LONDON   MELBOURNE   AUCKLAND

First published in Great Britain in 1962 by World's Work Ltd.
Reprinted 1989 by William Heinemann Ltd.

Text copyright © 1961 Else Holmelund Minarik
Illustrations © 1961 Maurice Sendak
0 434 94662 1

**Printed and bound in Great Britain by
William Clowes Limited, Beccles and London**

This I Can Read book is available from
Heinemann Educational Books, Halley Court, Jordan Hill,
Oxford, OX2 8EJ, as part of I Can Read Pack 2.

ISBN 435 00071 3

To all grandparents

and all grandchildren

CONTENTS

GRANDMOTHER AND GRANDFATHER BEAR

One day Little Bear went to visit

Grandmother and Grandfather Bear

in their little house

in the woods.

This was something Little Bear

liked to do.

He liked to look at all

the nice things,

the pictures,

Grandmother's flowers,

Grandfather's toy goblin that

jumped up and down in a jar.

He liked to put on Grandfather's
big hat and say, "Look at me!"
And he liked Grandmother's cooking
very, very much.

11

He had some bread and jam,

cake and biscuits,

milk and honey,

and an apple.

12

"Have some more," said Grandmother.

"Yes, thank you," said Little Bear.

"I am not eating too much, am I?"

"Oh no, no!" said his grandmother.

Then Grandfather said to Little Bear,

"We will have lots of fun today,

you and I."

"Yes," said Little Bear.

"But Father Bear told me

not to make you tired."

"Me—tired?" said Grandfather.

"How can you make me tired?

I am never tired!"

He got up and did a little jig.

"Never tired!" he said,

and sat down.

Little Bear laughed

and clapped his paws.

"Do you know what?" he said

to his grandmother and grandfather.

16

"What?" they asked.

"I like it here," said Little Bear.

He hugged them.

17

Little Bear and Grandfather

had all the fun they could think of.

Then Grandfather Bear sat down.

"Now we can have a story,"

said Little Bear.

18

"Good," said Grandfather Bear.

"Tell me a story."

"No!" Little Bear laughed.

"You tell me one."

"Then I must have my pipe,"

said Grandfather.

Little Bear ran into the house,

got the pipe, and ran back.

But there was Grandfather,

fast asleep!

"Oh—" said Little Bear.

He was sad, but not for long.

He went to look for his grandmother,

and found her in the garden.

Could Grandmother tell him a story?

Oh yes, she could.

She took Little Bear's paw.

"Let us go to the summer-house,"

she said. "It is cool there.

Come, Little Bear, let's skip!"

"Oh Grandmother." Little Bear laughed.

"How you skip!"

"You skip nicely too,"

said Grandmother.

They sat down in the summer-house.

Little Bear said,

"Tell me a story about Mother Bear,

when she was a little cub.

About Mother Bear and the robin.

I like that story."

"Very well," said Grandmother.

And so, she began.

23

MOTHER BEAR'S ROBIN

One spring day,

when Mother Bear was little,

she found a baby robin in the garden.

A baby robin, too little to fly.

"Oh, how sweet you are," she said.

"Where did you come from?"

"From my nest," said the robin.

"And where is your nest,

little robin?" asked Mother Bear.

"I think it is up there,"

said the robin.

No, that was a blue tit's nest.

"Perhaps it is over there,"
said the robin.

No, that was a swallow's nest.

Mother Bear looked everywhere,
but could not find a robin's nest.

"You can live with me," she said.
"You can be my robin."

She took the robin into the house,
and made a little home for it.

27

"Please put me by the window,"
said the robin.

"I like to look out at the trees
and the sky."

Mother Bear put it by the window.

"Oh," said the robin,

"it must be fun to fly out there."

"It will be fun to fly in here,

too," said Mother Bear.

The robin ate. It grew. It sang.

Soon it could fly.

It flew about the house.

And that was fun,

just as Mother Bear had said.

30

But then one day, it was unhappy.

Mother Bear asked,

"Why are you so sad, little robin?"

"I don't know," said the robin.

"My heart is sad."

31

"Sing a song," said Mother Bear.

"I cannot," said the robin.

"Fly about the house,"
said Mother Bear.

"I cannot," said the robin.

Mother Bear's eyes filled with tears.

She took the robin out

into the garden.

"I love you, little robin," she said.

"But I want you to be happy.

Fly away, if you wish.

You are free."

The robin flew, far up

into the blue sky.

It sang a high, sweet song.

Then down it came again,

right down to Mother Bear.

34

"Do not be sad," said the robin.

"I love you, too.

I must fly out into the world,

but I will come back.

Every year I will come back."

35

So Mother Bear kissed the robin,
and it flew away.

"And it came back, Grandmother,
didn't it?"

"Oh yes, Little Bear.
It came back.
And its children came back.
And its children's children—
here is one now."

"Ah—" said Little Bear.

"I would have let the robin

go free, too, Grandmother,

just as Mother Bear did."

37

"Hurrah!" cried Little Bear.

"Here is Grandfather."

"Then it is coffee time,"

said Grandmother.

She went into the house.

38

Grandfather looked at Little Bear.

Little Bear looked at Grandfather.

They both laughed.

"How about a goblin story?"

asked Little Bear.

39

"Yes, if you will hold my paw,"
said Grandfather.

"I will not be frightened,"
said Little Bear.

"No," said Grandfather Bear.
"But I may be frightened."

"Oh Grandfather!
Begin the story."

So Grandfather began.

GOBLIN STORY

One day a little goblin

went by an old cave.

It was old,

it was cold,

it was dark.

And something inside it went bump.

What was that?

BUMP!

"Hoo-ooh—" cried the goblin.

43

He was so frightened that he jumped

right out of his shoes.

Then he began to run.

Pit - pat - pit - pat - pit - pat—

What was that?

SOMETHING was running after him.

Oh my goodness, what could it be?

The goblin was too frightened to look back.

He ran faster than ever.

But so did the SOMETHING that went

pit - pat - pit - pat - pit - pat —

The goblin saw a hole in a tree.

He jumped inside to hide.

The pit - pat - pit - pat came closer,

closer—CLOSER— till it stopped,

right by the hole in the tree!

Then all was quiet.

Nothing happened.

Nothing.

The little goblin wanted to peep out.

It was so quiet.

Should he peep out?

Yes, he would. He WOULD peep out!

And he did.

"Eeeeeh—!" cried the goblin.

Do you know what he saw?

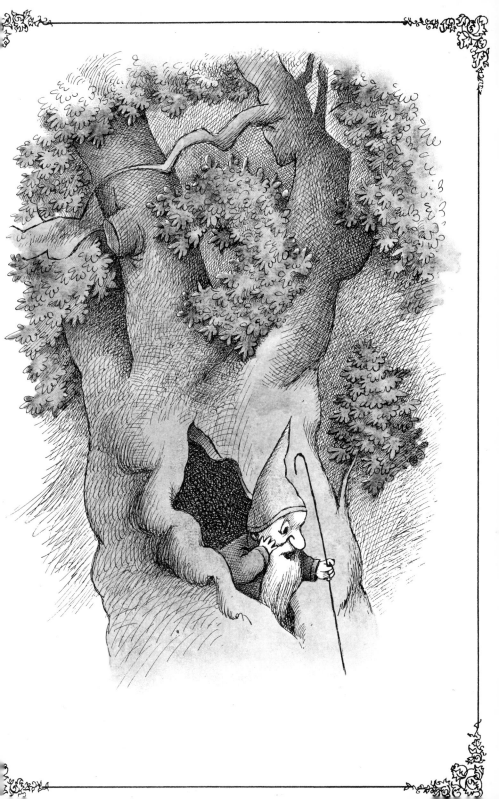

He saw— his SHOES!

His own little shoes

—and nothing more.

"Goodness," said the goblin,

hopping out of the tree.

"That old bump in the cave

made me jump right out of my shoes.

But they came running after me,

didn't they!

And here they are!"

51

He picked up his shoes,

hugged them,

and put them back on.

52

"Good little shoes," said the goblin.

"You didn't want to stay behind,

did you!" He laughed.

"Who cares about an old bump,
anyway," he said.
So he snapped his fingers,
and skipped away—

"—just like that!"
said Grandfather.

"I can't jump out of my shoes,"
said Little Bear,
"because I don't wear any."
He chuckled.
"That's how I like it."

NOT TIRED

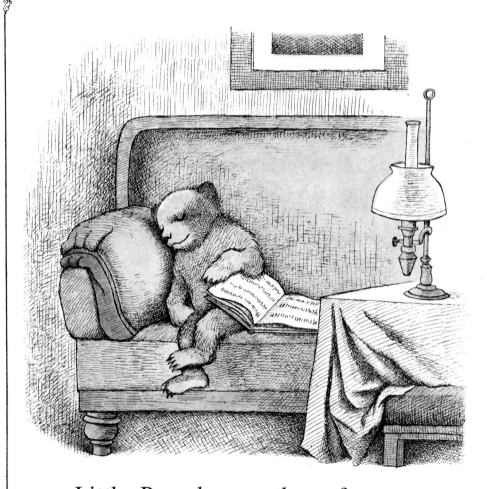

Little Bear lay on the sofa.

He was waiting for Mother Bear

and Father Bear to come

to take him home.

He said to himself,

"I am not tired.

I can shut my eyes,

but I will not go to sleep.

I am not at all tired."

He shut his eyes.

He heard a door open.

He heard Mother and Father Bear say

hello to Grandmother and Grandfather.

He heard them come to the sofa.

But he did not open his eyes.

"Ah," said Mother Bear.

"He is sleeping.

How sweet he is!"

Father picked up Little Bear and said,

"Yes, he is a fine little cub.

Tomorrow I will take him fishing."

"Look at him," said Grandmother.

"He is such a good little one."

59

"And clever, too," said Grandfather.

"Just like me."

They laughed.

Little Bear opened his eyes.

He said to Father Bear,

"Will you really take me fishing?"

"You scamp!" said Mother Bear

to Little Bear.

"You were not really asleep.

You heard about going fishing.

You heard all we said about you!

I can see it in your eyes!"

Little Bear chuckled.

He said to his grandfather,

"We had fun, didn't we?

And you are not tired,

are you, Grandfather?"

"Oh, no," said Grandfather Bear.

"A little cub like you,

and a grandfather like me,

we never get tired, do we?

We can sing and dance,

and run and play all day,

and never get tired."

Little Bear smiled.

He was growing sleepier
and sleepier.

Grandfather Bear went on,
"Yes, yes, yes! We can have
many good times, you and I.
But we never, never get tired!
You are not tired,
are you, Little Bear?

"Little Bear,"
said Grandfather,
"—are you tired?"

Little Bear was not tired!

No!

Little Bear was fast asleep.

64